"Here's a necklace for you, Nola,"
Gina said, giggling.
She pretended to loop the rope
over someone's head.
Then she staggered around,
making choking noises.

"*Ulk-ulk-ul-ul-ul-ulk-k-k!* This is the end," she gurgled. At last Gina threw the rope in the Dumpster and ran back up the path.

"Remember that," Monica said, crawling from the bushes. "Anyone who threatens Nola becomes another suspect."

She boosted Dee Ellen up the side of the Dumpster. "I see the rope," Dee Ellen said. "But it's way down at the bottom."

Dee Ellen leaned farther in. "I can't reach it—but wait—I've got something else. Wait till you see this," she said.

Dee Ellen straightened up. She held up a fuzzy-looking rag. "It's a *body*. The head's still in the Dumpster. And so are the insides."

"*What?*" Monica squealed.

"Somebody's desperate, all right," Dee Ellen said. "Somebody murdered Nola's teddy bear."

Books by Judith Hollands

Bowser the Beautiful
The Ketchup Sisters: The Rescue of the Red-Blooded Librarian
The Ketchup Sisters: The Deeds of the Desperate Campers
The Like Potion
The Nerve of Abbey Mars

Available from MINSTREL BOOKS

THE DEEDS OF THE DESPERATE CAMPERS

CHAPTER ONE

"I know you'll love it here at Camp Mini-ta-ha," said Mrs. Tully. She climbed into the Tullys' blue station wagon.

Monica Tully was standing in the camp parking lot with Dee Ellen Zeller. She hoped something exciting would happen here at camp. She hoped the Ketchup Sisters would find a case to solve. Something that would make them famous forever.

Mrs. Tully leaned through the car window. "I came here five times when I was a kid," she said.

"I remember it well," boomed Miss Glenda, the camp director. "Your mother, Sylvia Tully, was one of my very first campers."

Miss Glenda gave Monica a once-over look—for about the hundredth time that day. Monica was glad she'd wet down her bangs. Usually they flew around like dandelion fuzz.

"Here—don't forget this," said Mrs. Tully. She passed a photograph to Monica. It was a picture of the Tullys' dog, Zorro, sitting next to a steak bone.

"And this," said Monica's big sister, Page. She pushed a box of tissues through the window. "In case you get, you know . . ."

Monica's eyes bulged at Page's teasing face. "Homesick!" she cried. "You think I'm going to get homesick!"

Monica hated the way people forgot so fast. The Ketchup Sisters had helped catch a jewel thief. Now her own sister was back to treating her like a plain old kid.

"Mini-ta-ha campers are too busy to get homesick," Miss Glenda chirped. She gave Monica's shoulder a firm little squeeze.

"Just try to have fun," Mrs. Tully said. She started up the engine. "That's the important thing."

Miss Glenda turned to look at the girls as the car rolled down the driveway. "Your mother was a top-notch camper," she said to Monica. "Her name's still hanging in the lodge for winning the outdoor cook award. Do you have any of her talent?"

Monica shifted from foot to foot. She was thinking how her father broke a tooth on the popcorn she messed up in the microwave.

"Dee Ellen and I are detectives," Monica said. "We call ourselves the Ketchup Sisters."

Miss Glenda had a squashy hat pulled over her gray hair. "Detectives?" she said. Her bushy eyebrows did a little hop. "Imagine that."

Miss Glenda suddenly spotted some counselors carrying a raft. "You there—" she called as she scurried toward them. "Where are you going with that?"

Monica let out a big sigh. She was glad to be rid of Miss Glenda and her X-ray eyes.

"Welp, I guess we're really on vacation now," said Dee Ellen. She pushed her glasses up her nose.

"A good detective is always ready for action," Monica said crisply.

"Oh, okay," Dee Ellen said in a very unpeppy voice.

Monica eyed her partner. Letters on Dee Ellen's jacket said PORKY'S CHOICE PRIME BACON STRIPS. On the pocket was a picture of a pig in a tuxedo doing a jig.

A canteen hung around Dee Ellen's neck. "Aren't you supposed to be saving that for hikes?" Monica asked.

"Mom said to wear it all the time," Dee Ellen said. "So I'll be sure to drink lots of water."

Monica figured they'd be spending plenty of time at the latrines. That was the name for the camp toilets.

Dee Ellen pulled some little packets out of her pockets. "And I brought extra ketchup," she said. "In case they run out."

Monica just stared. Sometimes she couldn't help worrying. Dee Ellen had this habit of saying *yep* and *welp* all the time. And she hardly seemed to care about detective work. Now she was walking around in a dancing pig jacket. *Would she ever make it as a famous detective?*

A kid ran up to a counselor standing nearby. "Flower!" she shouted. "Some girl made Trudy cry. She said the bad kids get lowered down the latrines. Headfirst."

A girl with curly ponytails was sitting on the grass. Monica looked over and frowned. *Nola Abbott!* The only other kid in camp from home. And the biggest brat in town.

Monica and Dee Ellen followed Flower to the circle of girls on the grass.

"So when the kid starts to rot—" Nola was saying.

"Stop that!" Flower said, cutting Nola off. "How could you tell them a thing like that?"

A girl had her arm around a kid who was bunched up like a pretzel. "Now Trudy's got the hiccups," the girl said.

Miss Glenda popped up from somewhere. "Problems here, Flower?" she asked. She gave Flower her once-over look.

"I'm just trying to make friends," Nola whined.

Monica almost burst out laughing. "Nola always tells stories like that. She likes to make people squirm."

Miss Glenda looked first at Monica and then at Nola. "You two must know each other," she said. "Flower, put these girls in the same tent."

"Oh no . . . no, wait," Monica sputtered.

Miss Glenda gave Monica a stabbing gaze. All the other campers were looking, too. They were probably wondering what kind of kid would argue with the big boss.

"Never mind," Monica warbled, swallowing hard. The Ketchup Sisters were supposed to be trustworthy detectives. She couldn't spoil things by acting like a troublemaker.

Miss Glenda blew on her whistle. "Heave those bags," she called.

"You mean carry them *ourselves?*" Nola said. "But I've got more bags than anyone else!"

Monica stared at Nola's pile of stuff. The laundry bag was stuffed so full, it looked like a giant sausage.

"Mini-ta-has do most of the work around here," said Flower. "You'll just have to make more than one trip."

"Are you trying to kill me?" Nola wailed.

Trudy stumbled by with her friend Kim. She was still hiccuping. "That's a good—*hic!*—idea," she said.

CHAPTER TWO

Flower led a group of girls down a path and into the woods. On the way, they passed a wooden statue of an Indian girl facing the lake.

"That's Mini-ta-ha herself," Flower said. "People say a true Mini-ta-ha camper can hear her voice. She whispers her wisdom on the wind."

"A true Mini-ta-ha," Monica repeated. She looked at Dee Ellen. "That must be something like a top-notch camper."

"Here we are," Flower said, turning into a clearing. "This is our unit. There are ten units in camp and they all have names. Corky and I will be your counselors here at Tall Timbers."

"Tent two to your left," Corky called. "First come, first served."

Monica, Dee Ellen, and a blond girl named Lissy all climbed into the tent.

"I guess we'd better save a bed for Nola," Monica grumbled. "Miss Glenda said to."

Monica took her blanket and sheets out of her duffel bag. She began to stuff her pillow into a case.

"You've got a lot of nerve," hollered a voice from the back of the tent. "Now I'll be late for my own unit."

Monica pulled the flap open. Nola and a girl from Pioneer unit were facing each other. The girl dropped two of Nola's bags and scowled. "And don't think I believe you," the girl said, stomping off.

Nola ignored the girl and turned to tent two. "Hi," she called, smiling widely. Her ponytails were pulled so tight, her eyes looked squinty. She dragged her things into the tent. "Did I miss anything?" Nola asked.

"We're making up our beds," Monica said.

Nola dropped her puffy laundry bag onto her bed. "*Ourselves?*" she said again, letting out a big sigh. "Just think—we could be shopping in a mall right now."

Monica yanked at her sheet and a corner popped off the mattress. "You should get busy," she said. "We don't want to be the last tent ready."

Nola pulled her sheets from her tote bag. Then she took out a radio shaped like an Oreo cookie.

"You're not supposed to have radios," said Lissy. "It's against camp rules."

Nola made a horrible, squinty-eyed face. "You tell," she warned, "and I'll scream! I can scream for three hours straight. I've practiced."

Suddenly Nola spotted something on the tent above her. "A SPIDER!" she screamed. She hopped over to Lissy and stomped all over her sheets. "It could be a black widow!"

The spider was no bigger than a dot. "You're in the great outdoors now," Monica said. "You'll have to get used to a few bugs."

Nola stood watching them work on their beds. "Oh, no, I won't!" she cried. She jumped behind her bed and gave it a shove. "I'm *moving!*"

ER-ER-ERRRCCHH! Nola's bed began to bump toward Monica's end of the tent.

"You can't do that!" Monica cried. But Nola kept on shoving.

ER! ER! ER! ER! ER! Nola's bed and her bouncing laundry bag were headed right for her.

Suddenly Lissy shoved her bed, too. CLANK! The headboard crashed into Nola's. "You're not going anywhere," she growled.

"ROADBLOCK!" Monica shouted. She gave her bed a sideways push. CLANK! Nola couldn't get any farther now.

Nola's laundry bag popped open and all kinds of things tumbled out. Bracelets, belts, candy bars, bottles of nail polish, magazines, headbands—even a teddy bear.

"Hey," Nola cried, "look out for my stuff!" She climbed onto a mattress and began to leap from bed to bed.

Bompeta! Bompeta! Bompeta! Little colored balls started bouncing from the laundry bag. Dee Ellen's face lit up with excitement. "Did you bring Chinese checkers?" she cried. "That's my favorite game!"

"Those are gum balls, stupid," Nola said.

FWEET! The tent flap jerked open and Miss Glenda charged in, blowing her whistle. "What is going on here?" Miss Glenda boomed.

Her mouth opened up like a train tunnel as she turned from side to side. Tent two looked as if it had been bombed. "And candy!" Miss Glenda cried. She lifted a bag of candy bars from the tent floor. "That's strictly against camp rules!"

Flower was standing behind her. "I'll have them clean it all up," Flower said. "And throw the candy into the Dumpster."

"See to it," Miss Glenda ordered. "I never said this would be an easy job, Flower. I hope you can handle things here."

Miss Glenda's eyes were on Monica again. "I'd like to see you and your partner outside," she said. "Now."

Monica hung her head as Miss Glenda led them onto a path. *What could she think of Sylvia Tully's daughter now? Was she her all-time bottom-notch camper?*

Miss Glenda stopped and turned to face them. "Girls, I've got a detective job for you. I want you to keep an eye on Nola for me."

Monica couldn't believe it. Miss Glenda was giving the Ketchup Sisters a job! "You mean like spies?" she asked eagerly.

"More like special helpers," Miss Glenda said. "Some campers need extra help settling into camp life. I want you to keep Nola out of trouble. See that nothing happens to her. You can do that, can't you?"

The X-ray eyes were beating into Monica's body. "I guess so," she said weakly.

Miss Glenda whacked Monica on the back and smiled her gummy smile. "See?" she said. "You two just need a job to keep you busy. Everything will be fine now." She led them back to the tent.

They stood watching as Miss Glenda hiked away, humming the camp song.

"How about that?" Dee Ellen said. "She wants us to be nice to Nola! I feel like some kind of baby-sitter."

Monica felt pretty droopy, too. She'd been hoping for something a little more exciting. The Ketchup Sisters needed a really big case if they wanted to get famous.

"Wait a minute!" Monica cried. "We

can be Nola's *bodyguards!* That sounds better, doesn't it?"

"What do bodyguards do?" Dee Ellen asked.

"They protect a person from danger," Monica said. "From enemies, angry mobs—stuff like that."

Dee Ellen turned to climb back into the tent. "I wish I'd brought my Chinese checkers," she said.

Chapter Three

Corky and Flower caught Nola playing her radio. Nola said she couldn't sleep without it. The counselors talked it over and decided she could keep it.

Monica figured nobody wanted to put up with a wide-awake Nola all night.

The next morning Monica and Dee Ellen brushed their teeth at the outdoor faucet. "I wouldn't mind a rock station," Dee Ellen said. "But I think that was cha-cha music. That's the kind I hear in my dentist's office."

Nola stepped from the tent, looking half-awake. Flower had gotten her up early for hopper duty. The hoppers had to set the tables for breakfast up at the lodge.

"They are trying to kill me," Nola grumbled as she trudged down the path.

Dee Ellen wiped her glasses on the sleeve of her nightgown. Without them, she had nice, regular brown eyes. When she put the glasses back on, her eyes turned into big blurry blobs.

"Sorry I acted so poopy yesterday," Dee Ellen mumbled. There were big letters on the front of Dee Ellen's nightgown. The letters said I EAT AUNT GOODIE'S FROZEN DESSERTS.

Monica grinned and dumped the water from her drinking cup. "If we do a really good job, Miss Glenda will love us. Who knows? She might hang our names up in the lodge."

Dee Ellen wiped her mouth on her sleeve. "I don't think there's an award for best bodyguards," she said.

At eight o'clock, Tall Timbers hiked to the lodge for breakfast. But when they got there, Nola was missing. Tall Timbers' tables were the only ones with no dishes or silverware. Everybody stood around, wondering what to do.

Then Nola came slipping through a side door with a bread knife in her hand.

"*One knife?*" Corky said. "Don't you think we'll be needing more than that, Nola?"

"O-o-ops," Nola said. She dashed to the cupboards and came back with her arms full of silverware. "Help yourself," she said, dumping it onto the table.

"That kid gives me a big fat pain," Kim whispered to Trudy. "I'd like to fix her good."

After breakfast, a counselor named Ginger gave them archery lessons. Then they changed and hiked to the waterfront for swim tests.

"It's chilly this morning," the swim coach told them. "As soon as you're finished testing, you can return to your units."

Monica, Dee Ellen, and Nola passed the intermediate test. As they walked back by the lodge, Nola pointed at something.

"Look—a phone booth," she said. "I saw it there this morning. I'm going to call home and make my mother get me out of here."

"So go ahead," Monica said. She glared at Nola. "What's stopping you?"

"Because," Nola said, glaring back, "it costs ninety cents. All I brought is a five dollar bill."

"I didn't bring any money at all," said Dee Ellen. "My mother told me I wouldn't need any."

"Me either," said Monica.

Nola rolled her squinty eyes all around. "Great. Now where will I get the change?"

When they got back to the tent, Nola climbed in first. Then she let out a shriek. Monica and Dee Ellen scurried in after her.

Another bomb had hit. Nola's things looked as if they'd been blown around by a hurricane. Her suitcases were dumped upside down. The laundry bag was wadded up, empty, on the floor. Her pillow was popped open and the stuffing had been pulled out.

Nola turned the color of strawberry Jell-O. She flew to the tent flaps and whipped them both open. "Okay, who's the wise guy?" she yelled.

Lissy came hurrying up, shivering in her beach towel. "What's going on?" she said.

Now Nola was screaming through the back flaps. "Somebody wants their guts mashed up for gravy!"

"Oh, nothing," Monica said to Lissy. "Nola's just making new friends."

Chapter Four

Flower wasn't too happy when she got a look at tent two. "Another mess!" she cried. "Miss Glenda will explode if she sees this!"

Once again, tent two got a total cleanup. "Flower thinks we did this ourselves," Nola grumbled. "Did you hear what she said about a tentful of troublemakers?"

Monica fished a pair of Nola's underpants out of her rubber boot. Then she headed for the back tent flap. She made bulgy eyeballs at Dee Ellen.

Dee Ellen followed Monica out of the tent and down a path into the woods.

Bomp! The latrine door banged shut behind them. It was time for the Ketchup Sisters to have a private meeting.

"Who do you think did that to Nola's stuff?" Dee Ellen asked.

Monica squinted in the dim light. "Kim and Trudy are mad at Nola. If you ask me, it was them."

"Too bad Flower doesn't think so," Dee Ellen said.

"Flower will love us when we make them confess," Monica said. "It's time for some detective work, Dee Ellen."

"I hope we don't get as mixed up as last time," Dee Ellen moaned.

Monica flipped a toilet seat closed and sat down. "We started off too big last time—with a jewel robbery. A couple of troublemakers should be easy to catch."

BAMBA! BAMBA! Somebody knocked on the latrine door. "Everybody's leaving for the floating lunch," Lissy cried. "Flower says to come now."

Bomp! Monica and Dee Ellen hurried

outside to catch up with the line. "Keep your eyes on the suspects," Monica said in a low voice. "We've got to catch them before they try their next dirty little deed."

They all walked to the waterfront and stood on the dock. Tall Timbers was going to row onto the lake for a picnic lunch.

"Eat way out there?" Nola asked. "A kid could get seasick!"

Flower and Corky were checking the food in the cooler. "Trust us," Flower said. "That's never happened before."

Corky passed Flower a paper bag. "Put this in, too," she said. "You know me and my darn diet."

"But my ulcer," Nola said, clutching her stomach. "I'd better go stay at the nurse's cottage."

"She just wants to watch the nurse's TV," said Kim. She pushed Nola aside and climbed into the first boat.

Nola's eyes turned into squinty slits. She hopped in beside Kim and pushed up next to her on the seat. "I hope I *do* get sick," Nola said. "You should see what a person with ulcers throws up."

"Make her stop," begged Gina Conroy. "I can't stand stuff about people's insides."

"Your mother would have told us if you had ulcers," Corky said to Nola. "Come on, Monica. There's room in the front."

Monica stepped into Nola's boat. It seemed right. She could watch Kim and guard Nola's body at the same time. Dee Ellen got into another boat with Trudy.

"Shove off!" hollered Flower when all five boats were loaded. Monica's eyes slid over the faces in her boat. Nola was making her nostrils bulge at Kim. Kim was trying to ignore her. Corky was whistling and rowing the boat.

When they got to the center of the lake, the counselors tied the boats together. Then Corky did birdcalls and Flower taught them a finger puppet song. It was all about Old Man Tweet and his pet parakeet. "Tweet, Tweet, Tweet!" went everybody's finger parakeets.

"Time for lunch!" Corky finally called. Flower began to pass the bags from the cooler.

"Hey—" Nola said as she looked into her bag.

"More complaints, Nola?" Corky groaned.

Nola snapped the bag shut. "No—never mind," she said sweetly.

All the girls were quiet as they bit into their sandwiches. Corky and Flower were unwrapping little boxes of juice.

Suddenly Nola rose up from her seat. "*O-o-o-o,*" she moaned. "I feel sick." She stumbled sideways, falling onto Kim. "*O-o-o, uh-uh—bla-AHHH!*"

Kim's tan face turned pea green. "Nola threw up on me!" she squealed. Kim's hand flew to her mouth and she began to gag. "*Ulp-ulp—ERP!*" She pawed her way to the side of the boat. "*Erp-erp!—bla-*

AHHH!" Nola wasn't the only one losing her lunch.

"*Ee-eww!*" whined a voice. Gina's boat was tied up right next to theirs. Poor Gina had seen everything. "*Uh-uh-uh—bla-AHHHH!*" Gina ended up hanging right across from Kim.

"*Er-erp!—AHHHHH!*" Another head dropped as a kid pushed in beside Gina.

"GIRLS!" Flower shrieked. "NOT ALL ON THE SAME SIDE! YOU'LL TIP THE BOAT!"

The little party of boats was rocking like a bucking horse. Monica hung on for her life and kept her eyes closed. "*O-o-o. A-g-g-g. U-h-h.*" Moans came from everywhere as the boats rose and fell in the water. When the rocking slowed down, Monica opened one eye.

Corky was bending over Kim and talking in a soothing voice. Nola had slipped back up to the seat. She was sliding a lid onto a small round container.

"Hey!" Monica cried, jumping to her feet.

The boat started rocking again. "SIT DOWN!" everybody hollered.

Monica flopped back down. "But Nola isn't really sick! She just dumped cottage cheese in Kim's lap!"

Corky whirled to look at Flower. "Cottage cheese?" she said. "You must have given Nola my lunch bag!"

Gina lifted her head up from the next boat. "*U-h-h-h,*" she moaned. "I hate cottage cheese."

Then Gina slumped back over the edge of the boat.

Chapter Five

Somehow Tall Timbers made it back to shore. Corky sent Kim to the nurse. Everyone else headed back to the unit.

"I guess you're mad," Nola said to Flower. "Maybe you should send me home."

"Oh no," Flower said. "You'd like that. I'd have to think of something much worse."

"Like pulling her toenails off one by one?" said Lissy.

Flower nodded. "That's more like it."

Dee Ellen leaned close to Monica's ear. "Everybody's mad at Nola now," she whispered.

When they reached the unit, everyone stopped and stared. Something was very wrong with tent two.

"Our tent's caved in," Nola cried. "I could have been flattened!"

All the girls started mumbling to each other. "Oh brother . . . too bad . . . don't we wish . . ."

Flower held up a broken support rope. "This explains it," she said. "See? This rope was probably rotten."

"Maybe it was chewed by wild animals," Nola said.

"*E-ewww!*" Gina squealed.

"Must you always say something like that?" Flower asked Nola. "Now, everybody, go sit in the camp fire circle. Corky and I will fix the tent."

Dee Ellen was making bulgy eyes and bobbing her head toward the woods. Time for another meeting. Monica hurried down the pathway after her.

Bomp! The latrine door shut and they were alone.

"You call that some dirty little deed?" Dee Ellen cried. "We could have been in that tent, too!"

Monica dropped onto the toilet lid. "Do you think Kim and Trudy did that?"

Dee Ellen blinked and lifted one eyebrow. "Why not? Trudy has scissors—I saw them!"

Monica made a face. "Dee Ellen, those are toenail scissors. You'd need big, *big* scissors to cut that rope."

A corner of Dee Ellen's mouth twitched slightly. "Someone could cut it slowly. Little by little. In the middle of the night."

Monica tried to picture Trudy sawing away on the rope. In the black of night. Wearing her Tweety Bird nightgown.

"Now that's really crazy. Only a desperate person would do something like that," Monica said.

Dee Ellen leaned closer in the shadowy room. "Nola's making everybody desperate and crazy. She'll have a mob after her pretty soon."

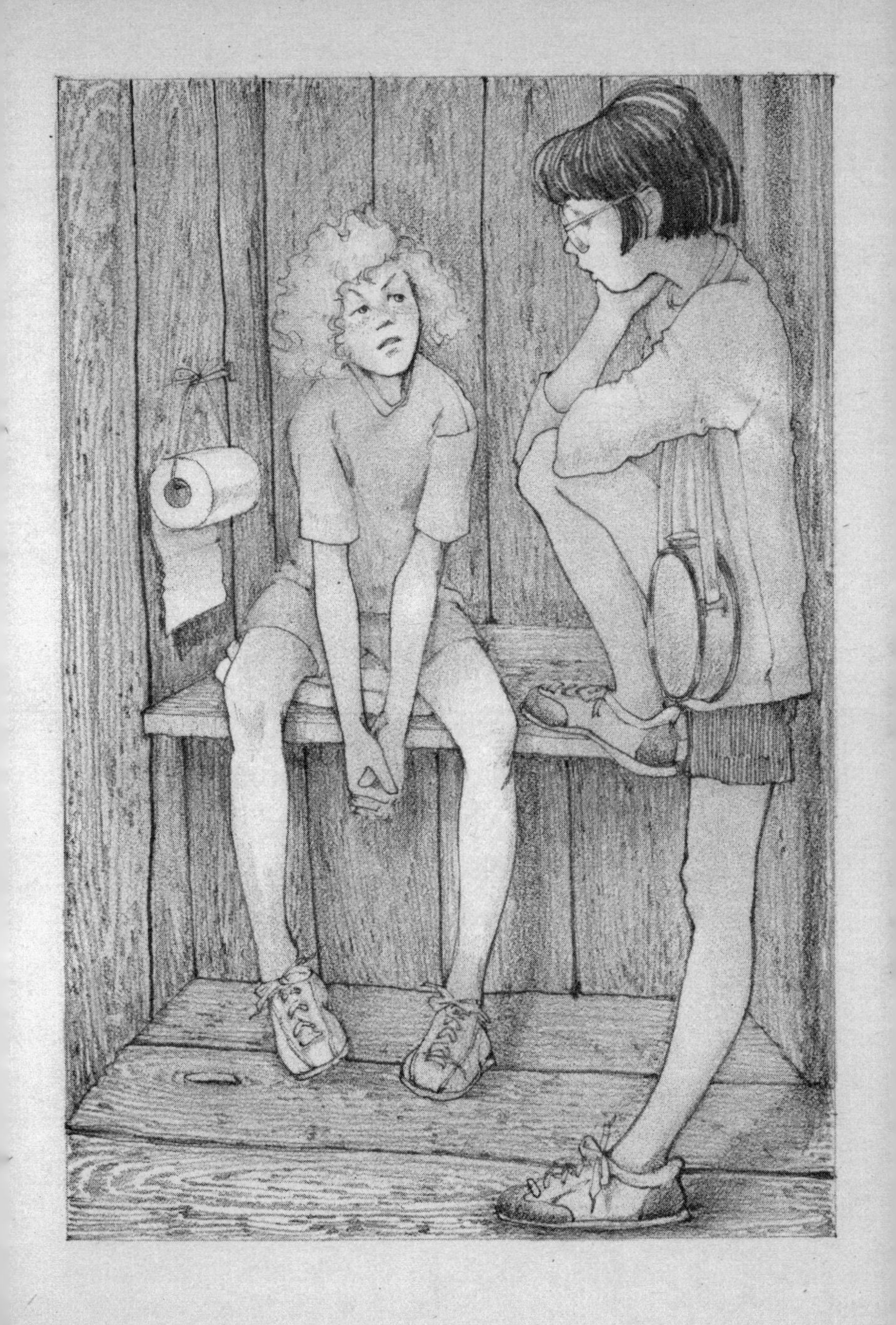

Monica stood up. "Okay. If it'll make you feel better, we'll take a look at that rope. Maybe we can tell if it's been cut."

BAMBA! BAMBA! BAMBA! Somebody knocked on the latrine door. "I hear you in there!" called a voice. "You're just talking."

"Flower will have someone throw the rope into the Dumpster," Monica whispered quickly. "We'll get it back out and inspect it."

"I GOTTA GO!" hollered the voice outside.

Monica opened the latrine door. A kid from tent three was waiting, looking very grumpy. "Keep your shirt on," Monica said. The girl stuck out her tongue as they hurried past her and into the woods.

The Dumpster was on a path nearby. Monica and Dee Ellen hid in some bushes and waited. Two girls from Pioneer unit came up and threw in a bag of trash.

"That's the girl who carried Nola's suitcases," Monica said. "She's mad at Nola, too."

"Nola didn't even thank her," said Dee Ellen.

They waited a little longer. Finally Gina came skipping down the path. She was swinging the piece of rope and talking to herself.

"Here's a necklace for you, Nola," Gina said, giggling. She pretended to loop the rope over someone's head. Then she staggered around, making choking noises.

"*Ulk-ulk-ul-ul-ul-ulk-k-k!* This is the end," Gina gurgled, crossing her eyes. At last she threw in the rope and ran back up the path.

"Remember that," Monica said, crawling from the bushes. "Anyone who threatens Nola becomes another suspect."

Monica boosted Dee Ellen up the side of the Dumpster. "I see the rope," Dee Ellen said. "But it's way down at the bottom."

Dee Ellen's bottom wiggled as she

leaned farther in. "I can't reach it—but wait—I've got something else."

Dee Ellen straightened up. "Wait until you see this," she said, dropping to the ground.

She held up a fuzzy-looking rag. "It's a *body*. The head's still in the Dumpster. And so are the insides."

"What?" Monica squealed.

"Somebody's desperate, all right," Dee Ellen said. "Somebody murdered Nola's teddy bear."

CHAPTER SIX

They stood looking at the teddy bear's poor ripped-up body.

"Nola hasn't even missed him," Dee Ellen said. "She's got too much other stuff."

A girl was skipping down the path. Dee Ellen quickly stuffed the bear's body into her jacket pocket.

"Hi," called a cheery voice. It was Nola. "I got the ninety cents," she chirped, waving a fist in the air. "I'm going to go call my mother now."

Monica watched as Nola disappeared down the path. "I wonder who gave her the money?" she said.

"Who cares?" Dee Ellen muttered. "If she goes, our troubles are over. We might even get to have some fun."

"But we're supposed to be guarding her!" Monica wailed. "What if somebody really desperate is after her? If anything happened, we'd be in big trouble!"

"Okay, okay," Dee Ellen grumbled. "We'll follow her. But I wish she would just go home."

When they got to the phone booth, Nola was nowhere in sight. Taped to the phone was a sign that said OUT OF ORDER.

Carlton, the handyman, was standing on the porch of the lodge. "That's broken, girls," he called. "Somebody saw a kid here this morning. She was sticking a knife down the coin slot."

Monica gulped as she remembered Nola and the bread knife. "S-some kid?" Monica stammered.

"Oh, I know who it was," Carlton said. "It's that brat from Tall Timbers." His eyebrows twisted up into angry knots.

"I'd like to get my hands on her, let me tell you."

"Another suspect," Dee Ellen said out of the corner of her mouth.

"Okay, you two," snapped a voice. "Just what do you think you're doing down here?"

Flower was standing beside them with her hands planted on her hips.

"We were following Nola," Monica began. "We didn't want anything to happen to her."

"I'm in charge of our girls," Flower said sternly. "Remember? I can't have you two wandering off whenever you feel like it. Miss Glenda is trusting me to do a good job."

Monica wanted to tell Flower that she was trying to do a job, too.

But Flower was in no mood to listen.

Chapter Seven

Nola sneaked back to Tall Timbers without being caught. But Flower sent Monica and Dee Ellen to bed early. Even after lights-out, Monica couldn't sleep. She lay there, listening to cha-cha music and thinking about everything.

A lot of people wanted to fix Nola Abbott. Could Nola be in danger?

How could the Ketchup Sisters keep Nola out of trouble? They were always in trouble themselves!

The next morning Flower made Monica and Dee Ellen scrub the latrine seats for an hour.

"Maybe they're all in it together," Dee

Ellen said. She dropped the scrub brush into the bucket. "Even Carlton. Maybe they're going to gang up and carry Nola away."

Monica picked up her bucket and headed back to the tent. "But why would they rip up her teddy bear?" Monica said.

"Desperate people do desperate deeds," Dee Ellen said. "They can't help themselves."

Somebody giggled from somewhere close by. Monica stopped walking and looked all around. Gina and Trudy were squatting behind a bush. They kept peering out at the back flap of tent two. Scattered in the other bushes were four more squatting girls.

"Oh no, Dee Ellen!" Monica moaned. She dropped the bucket with a CLANK! "You're right! A MOB HAS COME TO GET NOLA!"

"Don't do anything desperate!" Monica cried to the girls in the bushes. "You could pay for it the rest of your lives!"

"But we only paid fifteen cents," Trudy said.

Monica just stared. "Huh?" she said.

Gina pointed to tent two. "Nola said your tent was putting on a show before swimming. We each paid fifteen cents."

Suddenly the tent flap whipped open. "Tah-DAH!" Nola said, waving a hand toward the inside.

Lissy was standing by her bed, stark naked. Her mouth twisted into a lopsided shape. She snatched her bathing suit from the bed and tried to cover herself. "CLOSE THAT FLAP!" she screeched.

The kids in the bushes howled with laughter. "It would have been better," Nola called. "There were supposed to be two more kids in here."

Dee Ellen turned to look at Monica. "That's awful," she said.

"That's Nola," Monica answered. "That's how she got the ninety cents."

Nola took a flying leap from the tent. Lissy had pulled on her bathing suit in a

hurry. She was charging after Nola, snapping a towel like a whip.

"I'll kill her!" Lissy screamed. "I swear I will!"

"Crazy and desperate," Dee Ellen said. "We've got another suspect."

Nola ran right for them. Suddenly she stopped and pointed at Dee Ellen. "You . . . you," she sputtered, sounding like a stopped-up hose. "What did you do to Elmo?"

Monica and Dee Ellen looked down. Hanging from the pocket of Dee Ellen's jacket was a limp teddy bear's foot.

CHAPTER EIGHT

Flower was really fed up this time. She wouldn't even let them explain. She made all of tent two stay in and miss swimming.

Nola lay on her bed, looking extra grumpy. "This place is no fun," she said. "I can't call home. I should just run away."

Monica, Dee Ellen, and Lissy were lying on their beds, too. Lissy had her head turned, facing the tent.

Monica buried her head in her pillow. Nola was right. Camp hadn't turned out to be fun or exciting. The Ketchup Sisters were only famous for being two of the bad kids from tent two.

"You didn't have to rip up Elmo," Nola said to Dee Ellen. "I didn't know you could be so mean."

Monica sat bolt upright. "Dee Ellen didn't do that," she said. "We've been trying to find out who did! But we can't even make a move. Being your bodyguards is nothing but trouble."

"*Bodyguards?*" Nola said, wrinkling up her face. "Have you guys been guarding me? Well, you're doing a great job. A *tent* almost fell on me!"

Monica dragged herself across her bed on her knees, jabbing a finger at her chest. "It could have fallen on us, too," she said hotly. "Don't you ever think of anyone but yourself?"

Nola gave her a totally blank look. "Why should I do that?" she said.

A hand poked through the front flap. "Mail call," said a voice.

Monica rushed over. The girl from Pioneer unit was holding an armful of mail. "I see you guys are packed up for the sleep-out tonight,'' she said. ''Our unit's going, too.''

''Just give us our mail, Roberta,'' Nola said.

''You got a package,'' Roberta said to Nola in a snippy voice. She held a box up by its string. ''But I think it sprang a leak.''

Nola grabbed the box from Roberta's hand. Something powdery sifted from one corner.

''And a letter for everyone else,'' Roberta said. She passed the rest of them an envelope each. Monica, Dee Ellen, and Lissy sank onto their beds and tore open the letters.

''These are cookies from my Aunt Linda!'' Nola wailed. ''Somebody poked a hole in the box! I'll bet they put bugs in there. I'm not opening it!'' She tossed the box onto her bed.

''I think those are oatmeal cookie crumbs,'' Roberta said. She peered at the stuff sifting from one corner. ''At least you're not missing out on chocolate chips."

"Who asked you to be so nosy?" Nola said. She gave Roberta a nasty look.

"Touchy, touchy," said Roberta. She let the tent flap close with a *whap!*

"That does it!" Nola cried. "I've got to get out of here. I'm missing Double Dollar Days right now at the Big East Mall."

Dee Ellen looked up from her letter. "My mom just wrote me about it. They're giving free balloon rides to senior citizens."

Monica looked up from her letter, too. "And my sister and her friends are selling donut holes for the pep squad."

"And things are on sale!" Nola whined. "Everybody will be having fun and spending money but me."

"My dog had a tooth pulled," Lissy suddenly warbled. "I hope he's okay."

Everybody stared at her. A fat tear was rolling down her cheek. "He's been sleeping on my parents' bed,'' she blubbered. ''So he doesn't miss me so much.''

Lissy rolled to face the wall of the tent again. ''I sure miss my family,'' she said, sniffling loudly.

Monica's eyes shot to Nola. She'd made Lissy upset, and now she was homesick. ''I hope you're sorry,'' Monica snapped.

''Me?'' Nola said innocently. ''I don't even know her dog.''

Dee Ellen handed Lissy a box of tissues. Just looking at it made Monica think of home. A lump popped into her throat. *Oh no! Was she going to get homesick, too?*

''You just gave me an idea,'' Nola said, hopping up. She marched to the tent flap and jumped outside.

Dee Ellen got up and looked out after her. ''Do we have to follow her this time?'' she asked. The back of Dee Ellen's sweatshirt said APPLE-KISSED CIDER. Under the letters, a smiling apple was covered with lipstick kisses.

The lump was still in Monica's throat. She didn't feel like moving. "Let her go," she mumbled.

"Hey," Dee Ellen said. She lifted the box from Nola's bed. "Nola was right. Somebody did poke a hole in this box."

Monica got up and looked at it, too. Dee Ellen was peeping into the hole. "See any bugs?" Monica asked.

Dee Ellen's face went chalk white. "*Bugs?*" she said. She shoved the box at Monica. "Did somebody really put bugs in her cookies?"

Lissy still had her back to them. "Maybe they're just poisoned," she said.

CHAPTER NINE

Monica bolted out of the tent with the box in her hand. "Flower!" she shouted. "Flower! FLOWER!"

The camp truck was backing slowly into the Tall Timbers unit. Flower was waving her arms to show it how far to come.

Monica rushed up to her. "Somebody's after Nola," she hollered. "It could be a desperate person. These cookies could be poisoned!"

Flower gave Monica a long look. "You know, I don't get you," she said. "Can't you relax and have fun like the other girls?"

Most of the girls from the other tents had walked up. They had their sleeping bags in their arms.

"But Miss Glenda wanted us to guard Nola," Monica began. "And now Nola's gone. What if she's run away?"

A string of "*o-o-o*'s" rose up from the other girls. Then they began to whisper behind their hands.

Flower whirled to face them. "Don't anyone panic," she said firmly. "Nola is fine. She's with Miss Glenda right now."

When Flower turned back, she looked more than a little angry. "Nobody told me you were guarding anyone," she said. "If you ask me, this is all a big show."

She took a step closer to Monica and Dee Ellen. "Fun isn't enough for you two, is it? I think you want some extra attention for yourselves."

"No . . ." Monica began weakly. But her voice faded as Flower's words sank in.

Wasn't Flower sort of right? Hadn't

Monica been hoping for a lot of attention here at camp?

Flower snatched the cookie box from Monica's hands. "This is going into the Dumpster," she said. "And we're going to get back to business. No more tricks."

She turned and spoke in a loud voice. "I want all the sleeping bags piled into Carlton's truck right now. He's driving them to the overnight for us."

Flower lifted a finger and pointed it at Monica's nose. "And bring Nola's out, too. She'll be coming later with Miss Glenda."

Monica dragged herself back into the tent to get the sleeping bags.

"She hates us," Dee Ellen said miserably. "She thinks we're just big show-offs."

Lissy looked at them with wide eyes. "I didn't really mean it about the poison," she said.

"That's okay," Monica said. "I didn't have to start screaming. Nola's got us all acting crazy and desperate."

Monica and Dee Ellen hiked in silence all the way to the campsite on Pine Hill. When Tall Timbers arrived, Pioneer unit had everything ready for a hot dog roast.

"I'm not very hungry," Monica said to Dee Ellen. She tossed her half-eaten hot dog into a trash bag. "Let's go sit on those rocks up there."

They climbed partway up a hill. Dee Ellen dropped onto a big, flat rock. "I bet Nola told Miss Glenda we were awful bodyguards," Dee Ellen said.

"We are awful," Monica mumbled. "And awful detectives, too. We'll probably never know who did any of those things."

Dee Ellen sat studying her fingernails. "But we're still together," she said. "That's something. We promised to stay together forever, remember?"

Monica remembered. They'd promised that when they tried to be blood sisters. Only Dee Ellen hated blood. So they'd used ketchup instead.

APPLE
KISSE
CIDE
357

"Hey, you two!" Corky hollered up to them. "Come get your sleeping bags. The others already have theirs."

Dee Ellen and Monica made their way down to Carlton's truck. Monica climbed in and handed down the two bags. Then she stopped and stared.

"Dee Ellen," she said. "That other sleeping bag over there. Do you notice anything funny about it?"

"Somebody likes big yellow polka dots," Dee Ellen said.

"No," Monica said quickly. "Something else. If that's the last bag—then, why isn't it Nola's?"

Dee Ellen's mouth dropped open. "You're right!" she said. "Nola's has purple unicorns on it—not yellow spots."

Monica stood up in the back of the truck. She looked one way and then the other. "Somebody took it!" she said. "And there she is, carrying it into the woods!"

CHAPTER TEN

They hurried up the hillside as the girl with the bag slipped into the woods.

"Just a minute," Dee Ellen whispered when they reached the trees. She took off her canteen and held it up by the strap. "We might need a weapon. This could be a desperate person, you know."

There was another lump in Monica's throat. Dee Ellen could be a terrific partner sometimes. How could she have forgotten that so fast?

Monica choked down the lump and peered through the trees. A girl was standing within sight. She had dropped Nola's sleeping bag at her feet.

"Freeze!" Monica hollered, charging toward her.

The girl whirled to face them.

"It's Roberta!" Dee Ellen cried. "What are you doing with Nola's sleeping bag?"

Roberta burst into tears. "Nola promised me candy! I carried her suitcases. Then she said she didn't have any. She's got it somewhere. I know she's lying!"

Dee Ellen jabbed a pointed finger at Roberta. "You're the one who's been into her stuff! You ripped open her bear! You were looking for candy!"

Roberta nodded. "I can't stop thinking about a Choco-Crunchy Bar!" she wailed. "I can't even sleep!"

"Nola did have candy," Monica said. "But the counselors took it."

Roberta's body sort of wilted all over. Like cheese on a hot hamburger.

Suddenly it all made sense. "Roberta poked the hole in the cookie box!" Monica said. "To see if there was candy inside!"

"Yes," Roberta said pitifully. "My mom makes me come here for the exercise. But no candy—that's torture!"

Monica looked at Roberta. She was a desperate person, all right. She was a kid having a chocolate attack.

"Did you make our tent cave in?" Dee Ellen asked.

"Heck, no." Roberta said. "I didn't want to squash anyone. I just wanted a Choco-Crunchy Bar."

Monica turned to Dee Ellen. "I'll bet that rope was really rotten."

"Yep," said Dee Ellen. "It wasn't Carlton with his hedge trimmers."

"Carlton?" Roberta said, looking surprised. "What do you mean?"

"A lot of people threatened Nola," Monica said. "We thought one of them might do something awful."

Roberta twisted her fingers together. "I'll get her another bear. I'll send it to her in the mail."

"You bet you will," Monica said. "But

you're going to tell your whole story to Flower right now."

Roberta swiped a hand across her eyes. "Okay," she said, taking a step. Then she stopped and cocked her head. "There's that noise again," she said, looking from side to side. "Do you hear it?"

They all stood perfectly still, listening.

Monica looked down at Nola's sleeping bag. "Something's ticking," she said. "It's coming from the bag."

"*Ticking?*" Roberta's eyes got as round as pie plates. "Oh, my gosh! Carlton drove that bag here in his truck. What if he put something in it?"

"Now wait a minute—" Monica started to say.

But Roberta was off. She was running down the hillside screaming at the top of her lungs. "SOMEBODY HELP US!" she hollered. "HELP, HELP, SOMEBODY QUICK!"

Monica and Dee Ellen ran down after her.

"What is it, Roberta?" Flower asked, rushing up.

Roberta waved a hand toward the hillside. "Up there!" she shouted. "It's ticking! THERE'S A BOOBY-TRAPPED BAG ON THAT HILL!"

Girls crowded around as Flower made a face. "What?" Flower said. "I'd better go see."

Roberta dove for Flower's arm. "Don't go up there!" she begged. "What if it *explodes?*"

"EXPLODES?" everybody hollered. Most of the girls scattered like running ants.

"Flower, listen," Monica started to say.

"Not now, Monica," Flower said, waving her away. "I'll handle this."

"But, Flower," Monica went on. "I think I know why—"

Flower didn't let Monica finish. She turned to her with wide-open eyes. "You?" she said. "Is this one of your tricks?"

A yellow jeep pulled up and Miss Glenda hopped out. "Whatever is the matter here?" she said, eyeing them all.

Flower stammered and got red in the face. "We uh . . . had a report . . . uh . . . of something ticking . . . in a sleeping bag."

Miss Glenda's forehead rumpled up into bumps. "A *ticking* sleeping bag?" she repeated.

"I think we should call the National Guard," shouted one girl.

"Or the Mounties," said somebody else.

"I want to call my mother," wailed another voice.

"But it's not a booby trap," Monica said, stepping up to Miss Glenda. "Really. You'll see what I mean when it's nine o'clock."

Miss Glenda looked at her watch. "It's nine o'clock now," she said.

Monica heard a small *click* come from

up on the hillside. Then the sound of cha-cha music drifted down through the trees.

"Nola packed her radio," Monica said. "It's a clock, too. She sets it to turn on every night at nine o'clock."

CHAPTER ELEVEN

Flower and Miss Glenda took Roberta up to the big, flat rocks. Monica and Dee Ellen came, too.

Then Roberta told them all her whole story.

"So someone really was after Nola," Flower said. "And you two were guarding her."

"I guess I gave them that job," Miss Glenda said to Flower. "I had no idea they'd end up working so hard."

"We thought somebody might do something awful," Monica said. "Nola had everybody so mad."

Miss Glenda looked at the others down below. The counselors were helping the girls set up their sleeping bags.

"Take Roberta down with the rest," Miss Glenda said to Flower. "We can talk about repaying Nola tomorrow."

Roberta and Flower started down the hill.

"But where *is* Nola?" Monica said. "We thought she was coming with you."

Miss Glenda dropped onto a big rock and shook her head. "That child cried for three hours straight this afternoon. She wanted me to think she was homesick."

Dee Ellen swatted a mosquito that landed on her arm.

"But I know when a camper isn't going to work out," Miss Glenda went on. "Her mother came for her an hour ago."

Monica felt her mouth fall open. Nola had gone home! She was probably on her way to the mall right now!

Miss Glenda's X-ray eyes moved slowly over Monica and Dee Ellen.

"You two are detectives," Miss Glenda said at last. "Just as you said. And you're true Mini-ta-has too."

She pulled off her squashy hat and patted it against her chest. "The kind who care about people."

Monica looked away as her cheeks began to burn.

Miss Glenda hopped up from the rock. "Now get those sleeping bags set up," she boomed. "It's going to be a perfect night for stargazing."

Miss Glenda turned and started to march down to the others. She was humming the camp song to herself again.

"How about that?" Monica said as she and Dee Ellen went to get their bags. "Miss Glenda thinks we did a good job."

Dee Ellen headed back up to the rocks. "Let's sleep up there," she said. "I like that spot."

Monica followed and dropped her bag onto the grass. "Sleep?" she said. "I don't feel one bit sleepy. Can't you see what this all means?"

Dee Ellen was wriggling into her nightgown. "What?"

"It means the Ketchup Sisters are *getting better!*" Monica cried. She made super-bulgy eyes at her partner.

Dee Ellen stretched her arms and yawned. The front of her nightgown said SMILING SAM'S TOWER OF PIZZAS. "Yep," she said. "Maybe."

For once Monica didn't care if Dee Ellen sounded unpeppy. Or if she wore funny clothes. "Well, I know we are," Monica said. "We're better detectives, Dee Ellen. And true Mini-ta-has, too."

Dee Ellen climbed into her sleeping bag and rolled onto her stomach. Then she pulled herself up partway and slid her glasses onto the top of her head.

Monica sat hugging her knees and rocking back and forth. The sky was bright with stars and the moon was round and

orange. A breeze blew against her face. As it rustled through the trees, it sounded like a whispering voice.

Monica listened carefully. "And we're going to be famous, Dee Ellen," she added. "I know that now for sure."

Dee Ellen blinked. Her eyes were a nice shiny brown in the moonlight. "How can you be so sure?" she asked.

"Because," Monica answered. She lifted her cheek to the wind. "Mini-ta-ha told me."

About the Author and Illustrator

JUDITH HOLLANDS graduated from Boston University and has taught elementary school and gifted education. She says that she decided to write *The Ketchup Sisters* after she learned that "my daughter and her friend wanted to become blood sisters but neither of them wanted to deal with the blood. They came up with the idea of using ketchup and christened themselves 'The Ketchup Sisters.' I decided to jot down that title because it made me laugh. I told them then: 'I'll have to use that in a story.' " Ms. Hollands has also written *Bowser the Beautiful, The Nerve of Abbey Mars,* and *The Like Potion,* all available in Minstrel Books. She is married with two children, and owns two dogs, two cats, and three horses. The family recently moved to a thirty-three-acre horse farm.

DEE DE ROSA grew up in Colorado, graduated from Syracuse University, and now lives in a rural area of New York State. She is married and has two children, three horses, and one dog. Ms. de Rosa also illustrated *Bowser the Beautiful* and *The Nerve of Abbey Mars.*